MW00875148

THE
TREE HOUSE
CHILDREN

AN AFRICAN TALE

BY **CAROLYN WHITE**

ILLUSTRATED BY
CHRISTIANE KRÖMER

SIMON & SCHUSTER BOOKS FOR YOUNG READERS
Published by Simon & Schuster
New York London Toronto Sydney Tokyo Singapore

SIMON & SCHUSTER BOOKS FOR YOUNG READERS

Simon & Schuster Building, Rockefeller Center, 1230 Avenue of the Americas, New York, New York 10020. Text copyright
© 1994 by Carolyn White. Illustrations copyright © 1994 by Christiane Krömer. All rights reserved including the right of
reproduction in whole or in part in any form. SIMON & SCHUSTER BOOKS FOR YOUNG READERS is a trademark of Simon &
Schuster. Designed by Vicki Kalajian. The text for this book is set in Cloister. The illustrations were done in watercolor.
Manufactured in the United States of America.   10   9   8   7   6   5   4   3   2   1

Library of Congress Cataloging-in-Publication Data

White, Carolyn. The tree house children / by Carolyn White; illustrated by Christiane Krömer. Summary: In a fisherman's
absence a hungry witch tries to get into his house up in a baobab tree, where his children are playing. [1. Folklore — Africa.]
I. Krömer, Christiane, ill.   II. Title. PZ8.1.W584Ch   1994   398.21 — dc20   [E]   CIP   92-46428   ISBN 0-671-79818-9

For Win, who's not afraid of witches — CW

To John Gundelfinger — CK

A fisherman had two children. He built
them a house in a baobab tree. He made a
rope ladder from the bark.

"I am going fishing now, children," said the fisherman. "Stay in the tree house. And don't drop the ladder down to anybody but me."

All day the children played in the tree
house while their father, with hooks on
a line, fished in the river.

At night when his gourd was filled with fish, he
came home to the tree. He called out to his children:
"Children, children, in the tree,
drop the ladder down to me."

The children dropped the ladder down. Their
father climbed up the tree. He cooked fish for his
children. When the children were sleepy, they lay
down on the same mat to sleep.

Next morning the fisherman again went fishing. "Don't drop the ladder down to anybody but me," the father warned his children.

At night, after he had caught lots of fish, the father came back to the tree and called:

> "Children, children, in the tree,
> drop the ladder down to me."

The children dropped the ladder down. Their father climbed up the tree.

Now a witch was walking by the baobab. She
saw the children drop the ladder down. She saw the
father climb up the tree.

"Oh, ho," said the witch. "Tomorrow I shall eat
those children."

And rushing to an anthill,
she licked the ants and
let them bite her tongue
so that it swelled
to a great size.

Next morning
the fisherman again
went fishing. "Don't drop
the ladder down to anybody
but me," said the father to his
children. All morning the children
played in the tree house.
The witch stood under the tree.
With her swollen tongue, she called
out in a voice just like their father's:
"Children, children, in the tree,
drop the ladder down to me."

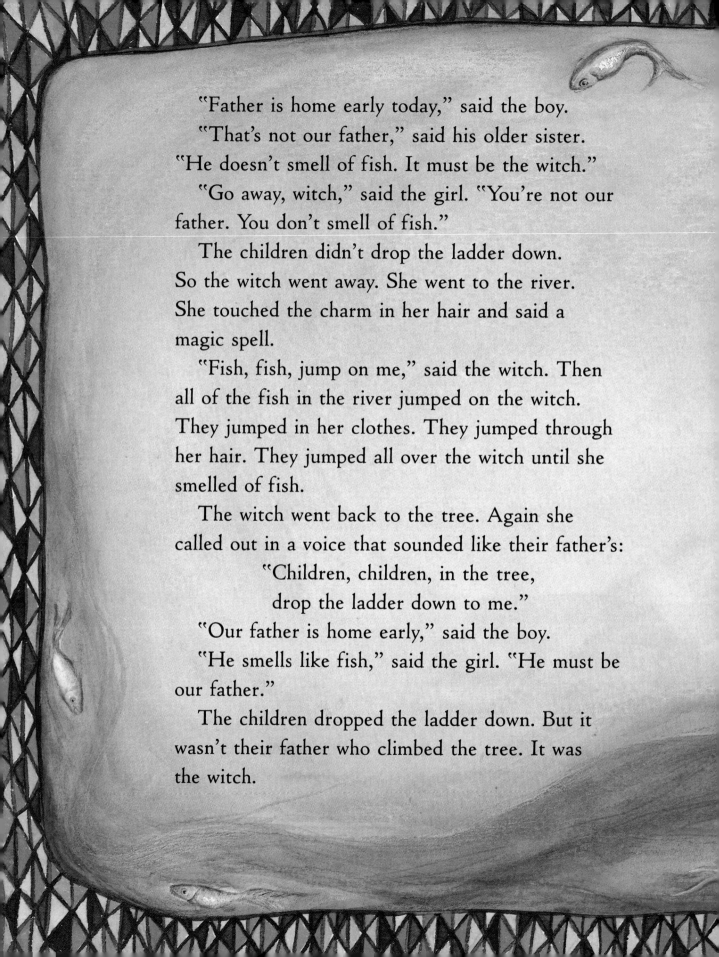

"Father is home early today," said the boy.

"That's not our father," said his older sister. "He doesn't smell of fish. It must be the witch."

"Go away, witch," said the girl. "You're not our father. You don't smell of fish."

The children didn't drop the ladder down. So the witch went away. She went to the river. She touched the charm in her hair and said a magic spell.

"Fish, fish, jump on me," said the witch. Then all of the fish in the river jumped on the witch. They jumped in her clothes. They jumped through her hair. They jumped all over the witch until she smelled of fish.

The witch went back to the tree. Again she called out in a voice that sounded like their father's:
    "Children, children, in the tree,
        drop the ladder down to me."

"Our father is home early," said the boy.

"He smells like fish," said the girl. "He must be our father."

The children dropped the ladder down. But it wasn't their father who climbed the tree. It was the witch.

The witch grabbed the children. She tucked the
boy under the left side of her waist cloth, she tucked
the girl under the right, and slid down the tree.

"Help, Father!" cried the children.

Now the father, coming home from the river,
heard his children cry. He saw the witch running,
the children tucked under her waist cloth.

So he ran after them, the gourd full of fish balanced on his head.

The witch ran home. She set a big pot of water to boil. She chopped hot chili peppers and put them in the pot.

"The witch wants to eat my children," said the father. "I must save them."

The father climbed up a tree.
He looked down on the witch,
who was stirring the pot.
Caught under her waist cloth
were the children.

Quietly, the father dropped
a hook down to the left side of
the witch. He fished the boy up.
He pulled the boy safely up
into the tree.

"*Shhh!*" said the father.
"Don't let the witch hear you."

The father
dropped a hook down
to the witch's right side.
He pulled the girl
safely up into the tree.
"*Shhh!*" said the father.
"The witch mustn't hear us."
Into the witch's waist cloth
he dropped two live fish.
The father and his children
sneaked down from the tree.
They ran back home to their tree
house. They climbed up their
ladder. They were safe.
Now the fish in the witch's
waist cloth began wiggling. They
began wiggling like children.

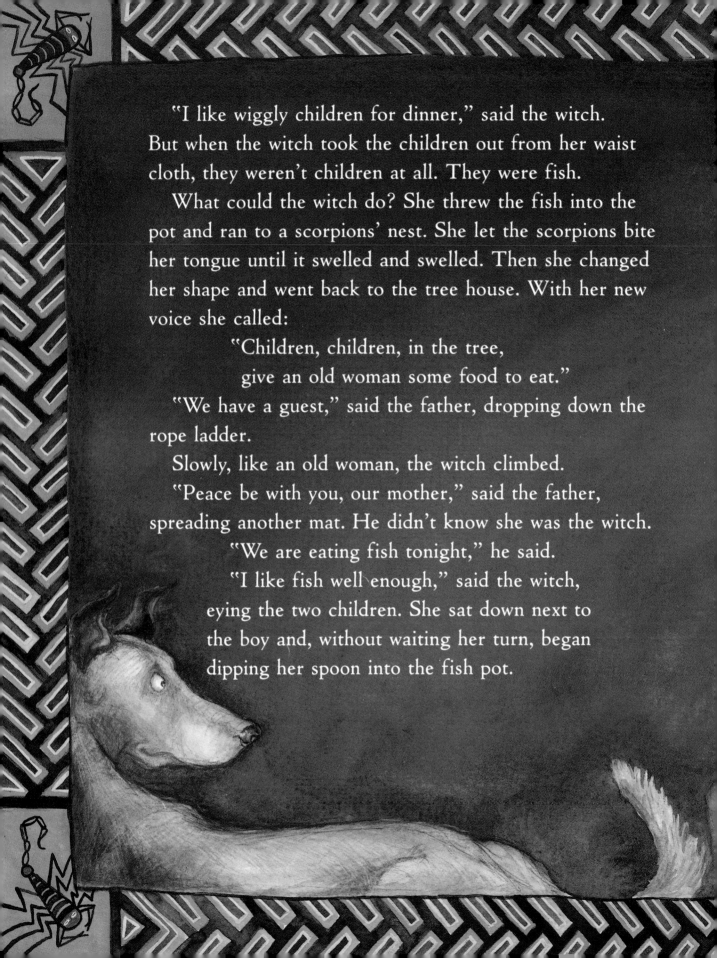

"I like wiggly children for dinner," said the witch. But when the witch took the children out from her waist cloth, they weren't children at all. They were fish.

What could the witch do? She threw the fish into the pot and ran to a scorpions' nest. She let the scorpions bite her tongue until it swelled and swelled. Then she changed her shape and went back to the tree house. With her new voice she called:

"Children, children, in the tree,
give an old woman some food to eat."

"We have a guest," said the father, dropping down the rope ladder.

Slowly, like an old woman, the witch climbed.

"Peace be with you, our mother," said the father, spreading another mat. He didn't know she was the witch.

"We are eating fish tonight," he said.

"I like fish well enough," said the witch, eying the two children. She sat down next to the boy and, without waiting her turn, began dipping her spoon into the fish pot.

She ate and she ate. She ate with both hands.

"She's not an old woman," the girl whispered to her brother. "Look how greedy she is. She's the witch. She'll eat us next."

So the girl slipped a fishhook into the
witch's bowl. The witch gobbled it up.

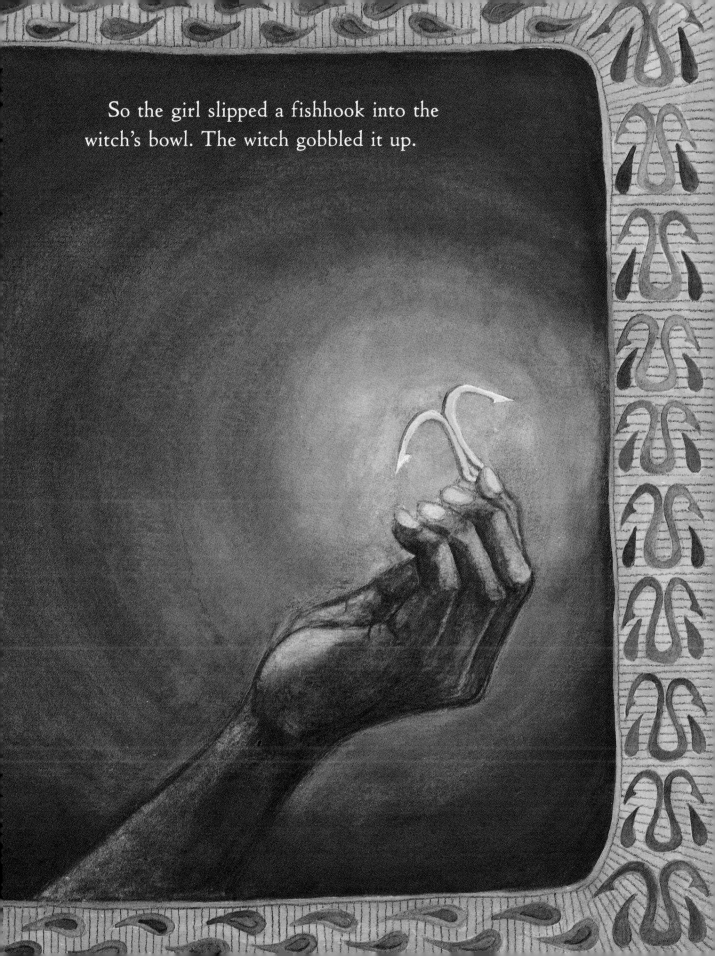

"I am dying," she cried as the fishhook pierced her heart. "When I am dead," the witch told the girl, "you must cut the charm from my hair and throw it into the fire. Then all the children I have eaten will come back alive."

With a shudder, the witch fell dead. And before the witch turned to dust, the girl cut the charm from the witch's hair and threw it into the fire.

At once the tree house was filled with children.
They were happy to be alive.
And they were very hungry.
"You are welcome," said the father to the
children, "to share what's left of our supper."

So the children sat down on the mats and in
turn dipped their spoons into the fish pot. Then they
dipped their spoons again until each child had
plenty of fish stew. And when the children grew
sleepy, they lay down on the mats close to the sister
and brother. Tired, they fell asleep fast.

That night an owl in the baobab counted nearly as many children asleep in the tree house as there are stars in the sky.